W9-CCR-522

U WHISPER
IN MY EAR
I LOVE U WHILE
I SING A SOFT
MELODY TO
SAY GOODBYE.

For my dad and mom,
and for Tulsi and Narayan Blue, with love

A special nod to one of our family's favorite books, *I Lost My Tooth in Africa*, created by Baba Wagué Diakité and his daughter, Penda, which taught us about the African tooth fairy.

Henry Holt and Company, *Publishers since 1866*
Henry Holt® is a registered trademark of Macmillan Publishing Group, LLC
120 Broadway, New York, NY 10271
mackids.com

Library of Congress Cataloging-in-Publication Data
Names: Kostecki-Shaw, Jenny Sue, author, illustrator.
Title: Papa brings me the world / Jenny Sue Kostecki-Shaw.
Description: First edition. | New York : Henry Holt and Company, 2020. | "Christy Ottaviano Books." | Audience: Ages 4–8. | Audience: Grades K–1. | Summary: Even though he brings exotic gifts home when he returns, a young girl misses her father, who travels around the world as a photojournalist.
Identifiers: LCCN 2019039528 | ISBN 9781250159250 (hardcover)
Subjects: CYAC: Fathers and daughters—Fiction. | Separation (Psychology)—Fiction. | Travel—Fiction.
Classification: LCC PZ7.K85278 Pap 2020 | DDC [E]—dc23
LC record available at https://lccn.loc.gov/2019039528

First edition, 2020 / Designed by Mallory Grigg
Acrylics, watercolors, salt, pencil, rubber stamps, and collage on Strathmore illustration board were used to create the art for this book.

Printed in China by RR Donnelley Asia Printing Solutions Ltd., Dongguan City, Guangdong Province
1 3 5 7 9 10 8 6 4 2

Christy Ottaviano Books
Henry Holt and Company
New York

When Papa goes to work, I sneak tiny love notes into his pockets. He kisses my wet cheeks and says, “Mmmmmmmm, salty. You taste like the Indian Ocean.” *He* would know.

Most parents drive a car or ride a bus or train to work—but not my papa.

He navigates mountains, deserts, and oceans.

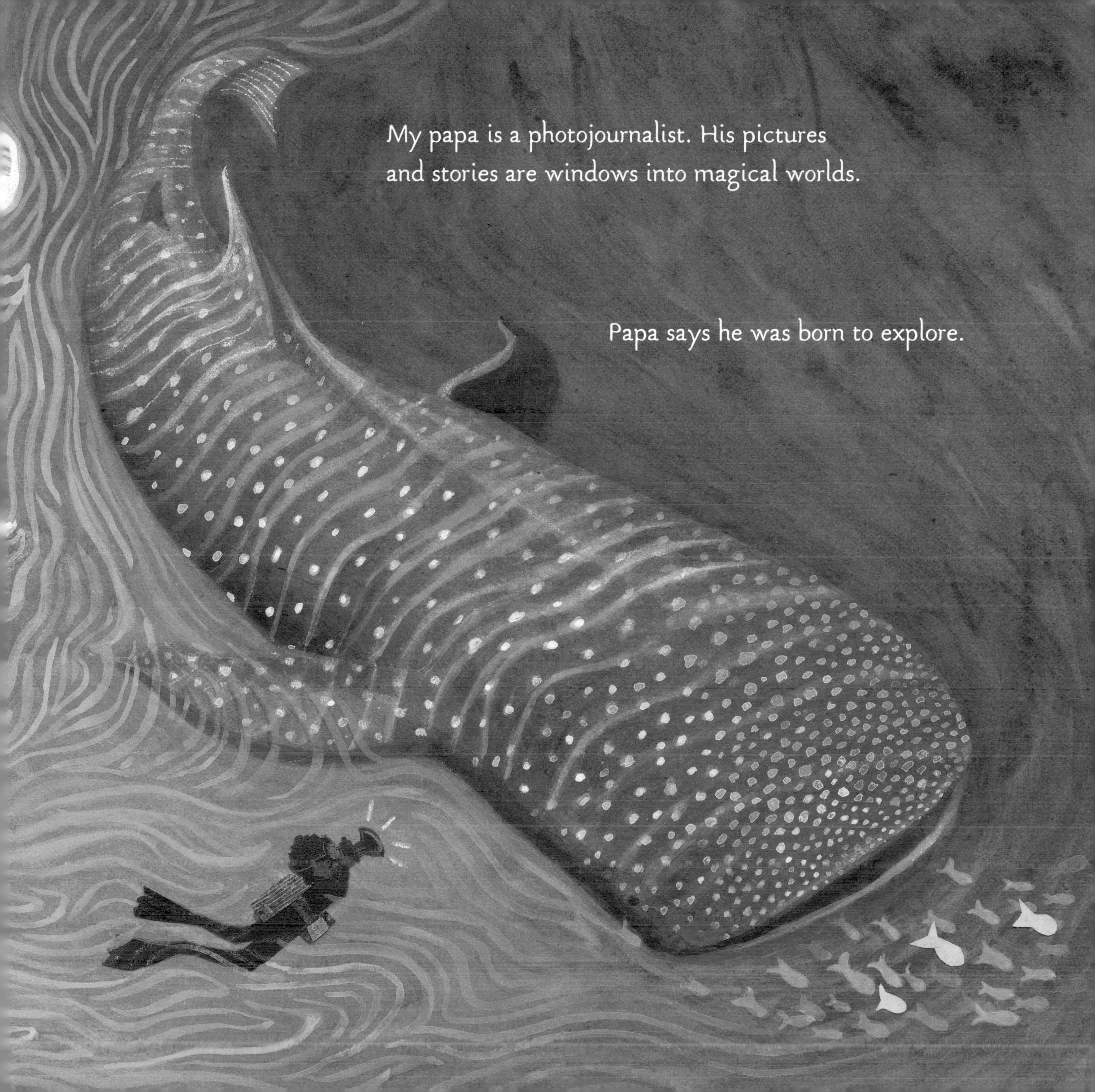

My papa is a photojournalist. His pictures and stories are windows into magical worlds.

Papa says he was born to explore.

When Papa comes home, his pockets are treasure troves of silver and gold!

I have coins from twenty-eight countries—the ones with holes are my favorites.

"Papa, I'm saving up for a ticket around the world!"

"People haven't always used coins or paper money," Papa replies.
"In Cameroon, people once bartered with potato mashers!"

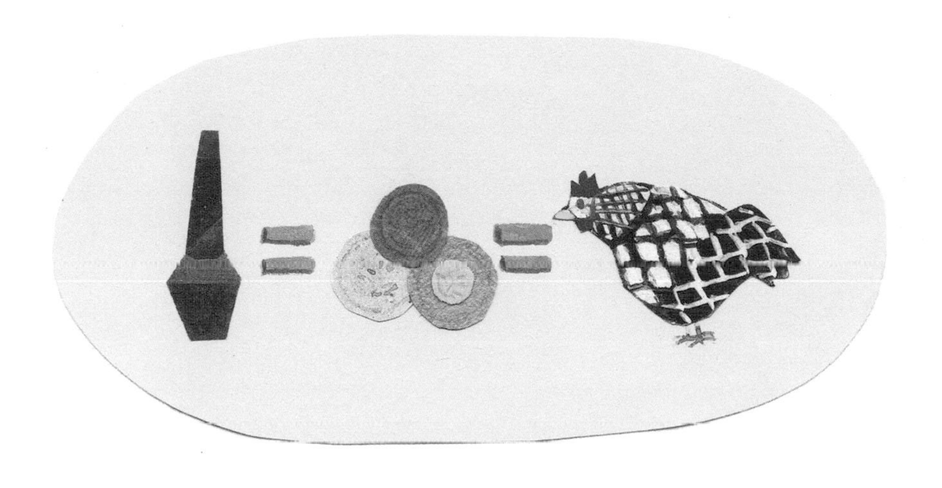

"I'm coming with you!" I declare.

Papa's eyebrows stand tall like openings to caves.

"Someday, Lu," he says, "but until then, I'll bring the world to you."

Papa found this ancient calculator
in China. It doesn't even have numbers!

Tonight, Mama and I
count the stars—
and the days until
Papa comes home.

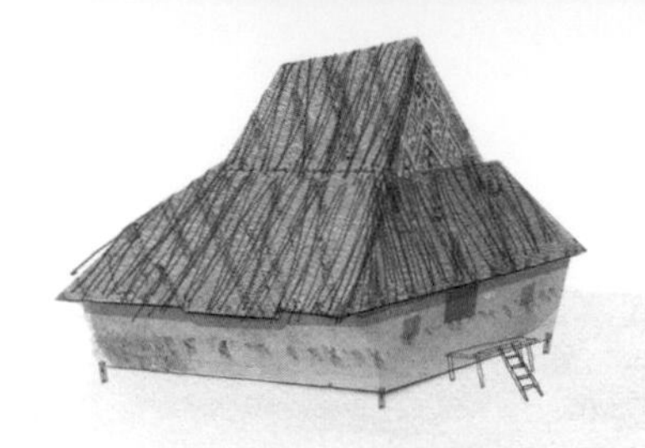

When Papa returns, he
teaches me a game that
children in Sumatra taught him.
It's called *Semut, Orang, Gajah.*
Ant, Person, Elephant.

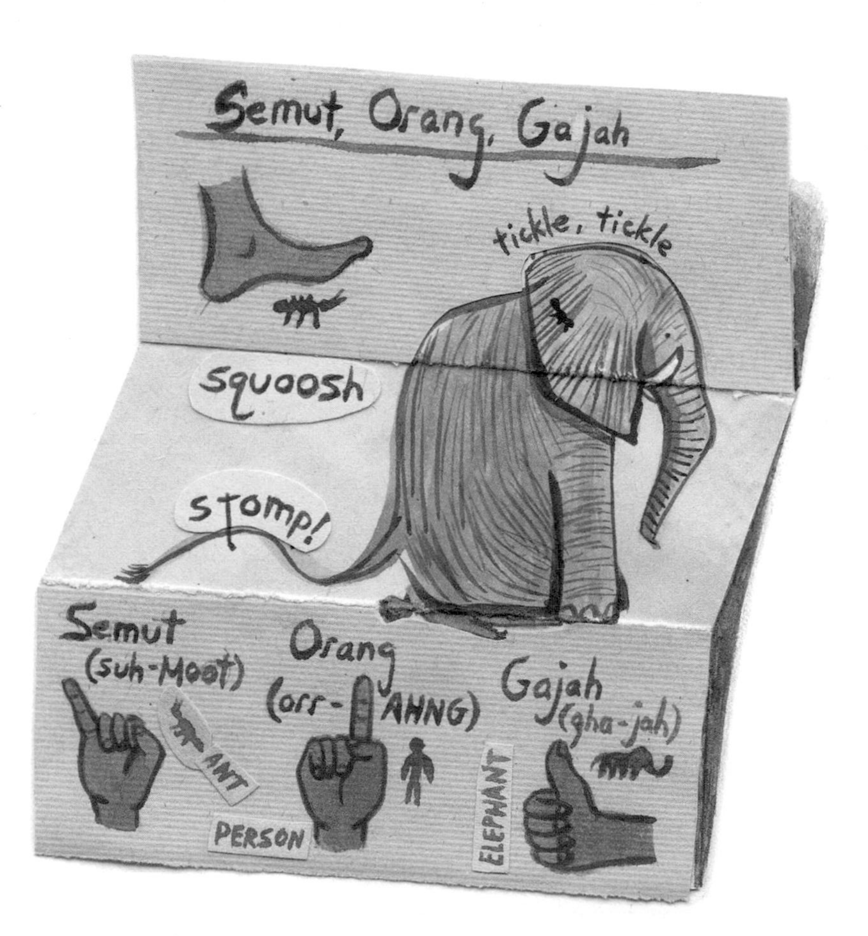

"It's like Rock, Paper,
Scissors," Papa says.
"Same-same but different!
Best out of three?"

"If I win, will you take me
on your next adventure?"

Papa smiles. "Someday, Lu."

Papa hauled a piano
all the way back from
Africa—IN HIS SOCK!
His friend made this
mbira, or thumb piano,
so I could hear the sounds
of Zimbabwe.

I think it sounds
like birdsong.

Papa fills his journals with everything he sees. I imagine me in his pages.

International Kite Festival
Ahmedabad
Gujarat India
"Uttarayan"
INDIA
Canada
BUDDHA
asil's Cathedral, Moscow, Russia

Mama and I cover the wall with a giant map of the world to keep track of Papa. She asks me where I want to explore.

"Everywhere!" I shout, stretching my arms across the oceans.

Some nights, Papa feels as far away as the moon.

I try to dream myself to sleep. Tonight, I am dancing flamenco with flamingos in the South of France.

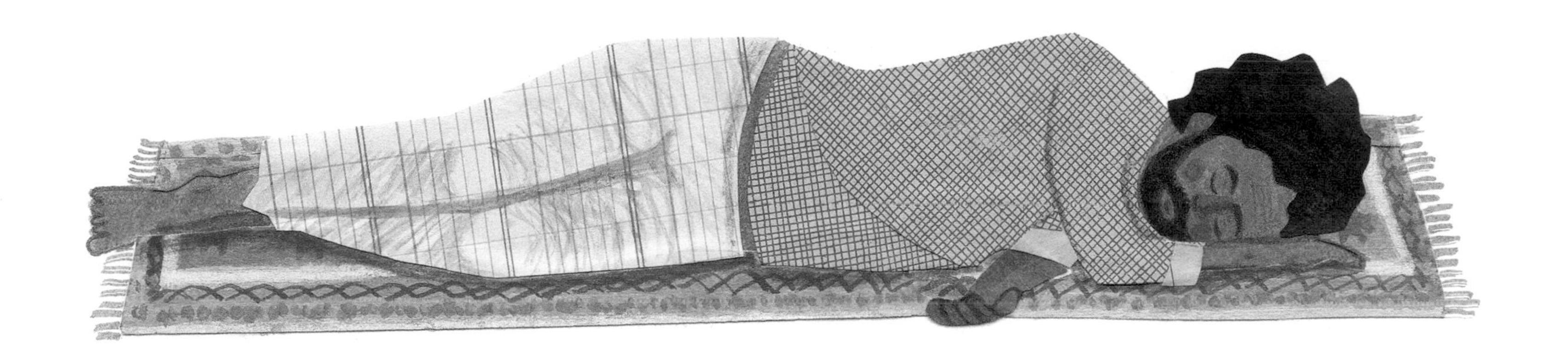

I wonder what Papa's world looks like right now.
Is he trying to fall asleep like me?

I hear him whisper,
"*Lala salama*, Lu. Sleep peacefully."

Other days, Papa seems as close
as a cloud that I can almost touch,
like the day he sent me
a new friend in the mail!

Dear Lulu,
My name is Miguel. Your papá
and my papá are new friends!
We live in the jungle in Yucatán,
Mexico. If you come to my village,
you will sleep in a rainbow-colored
hammock, and my mamá will
grind cacao beans to make hot
chocolate. What is it like where
you live? Do you play fútbol?
Do you speak español?
Will you visit us someday?
Adiós, mi amiga.
Goodbye, my friend.
– Miguel

Papa says, “When you keep
your eyes and heart wide open,
new friends await you
wherever you go.”

Papa comes home while I'm sleeping and kisses me on the forehead. I know it's Papa. He smells sweet and salty. Like the world.

“I befriended this driftwood dragon at
a beach on the Irish Sea,” Papa whispers.

My fingers sail up and down its smooth bumps.
“I wish we could fly on its
back together!”

"I'm hungry," I say, "for one of your stories!"

"Hmm." (He always begins that way.) "Once . . . I was trekking in the Andes Mountains, playing peekaboo with a rare bird, and I meandered off the trail. Suddenly, a mischievous fog snuck in, leaving me standing alone in a cloud. Everywhere I turned was white. My heart pounded. I was lost.

"Then, out of nowhere, I spied
a pile of rocks, called a cairn,
pointing the way."

"I didn't know papas
got scared," I say.

Papa sighs. "Sure, sometimes."

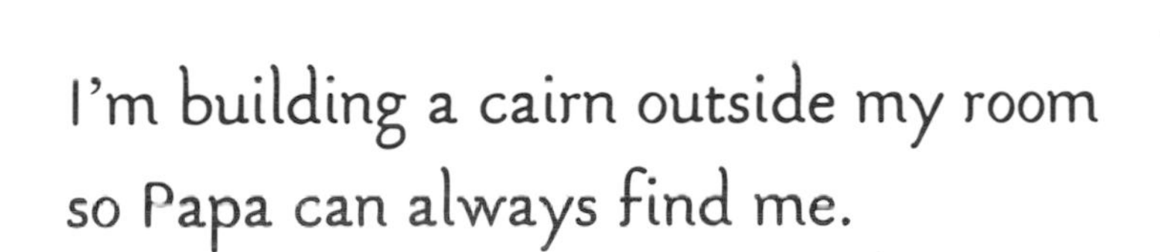

I'm building a cairn outside my room
so Papa can always find me.

When he's homesick, Papa says my messages are the best medicine.

Dear Papa,
I lost my first tooth! I put it under the calabash gourd you brought back from Mali, and the tooth fairy left me two chicks!
Love, Lu
P.S. I named them Queen Frittata and Roo.

Dear Lu,
Wow! The African tooth fairy visited you?! Say hi to Queen Frittata and Roo for me, and please don't lose another tooth before I get home. Can't wait to see your new smile.
Love, Papa
P.S. Look for a package from Turkey!

Today was my school play. I rubbed the magic lamp Papa sent until my hand tingled hot, wishing he would appear.

I love treasures,

but I'd rather have Papa.

Papa comes and goes.
It's his nature.
I'm just happy he's here today.

"Close your eyes, Lu," Papa says, and places a surprise in my hands. *It's a book.*

"But, Papa," I say, "it's blank."

"It's time." He winks.

"Time for what?" I ask.

"Time for you to fill your own pages!"

Mama helps me pack
everything I'll need.

Finally, *someday* is here, and I'm crossing the oceans, *with* Papa.

Together, we step
into a wide world.

And I fill my journal with everything I see.

A flying fox is NOT a fox!
It's a fruit bat!
Papa and I volunteered
at a center for sick and
injured animals and
I got to bottle-feed a
baby flying fox!
This is my new friend Alkira. Her family has lived in Australia for 65000 years!
yellow tail flowers
I call it
purple pinwheel.
Christmas
bells
Eucalyptus seedpod

I was born to explore.

Just like Papa.

circa 1980

Ceramic bird from South Africa

Coins my dad brought home

my Belgium pen pal

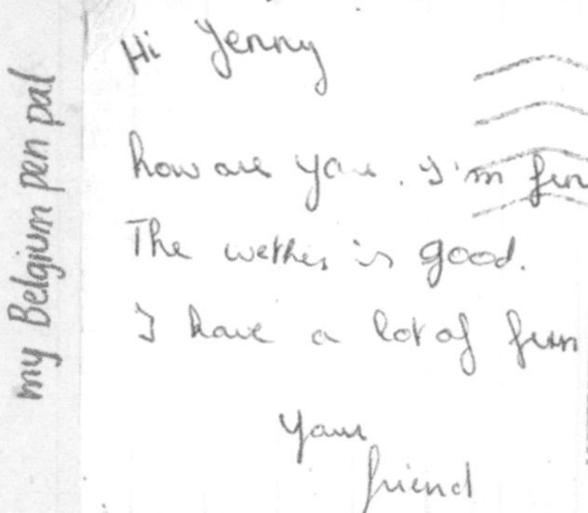

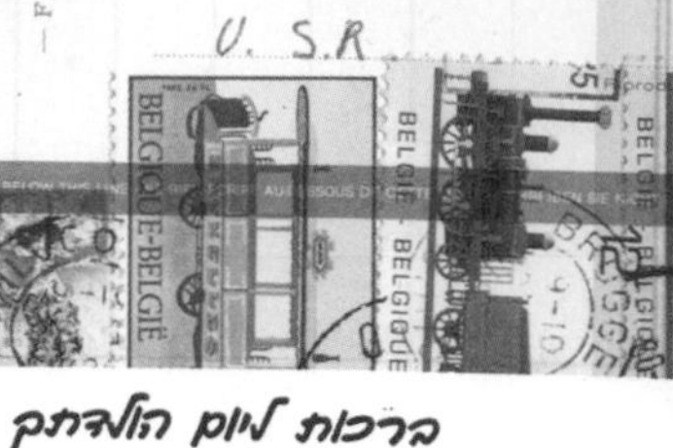

Author's Note

When I was young, my dad's work led him around the world. My sister and brothers and I tucked homemade cards in his suitcase. With Mom's help, we followed his journeys (and learned geography) on a giant map of the world that hung on the kitchen wall. My dad worked hard to help others and to provide for our family. Still, I remember feeling sad because I missed him.

Of all the gifts Dad carried home, I loved his stories the most. Stories of being a guest in remote villages where smiling was the shared language. Tales of graceful giraffes walking in sync alongside his car, of visiting a man who lived in a medieval castle. With every treasure, my curiosity for the world grew. I longed to go with him! "*Someday*," he'd reply.

That *someday* eventually came when we traveled to Australia together. It was a gift from my parents. Dad and I visited the Three Sisters Rock Formation in the Blue Mountains. We ran five miles in the pouring rain along Sydney Harbor and up the steps of the Sydney Opera House. We listened to an Aboriginal man play the didgeridoo and met a wombat in a eucalyptus forest. We visited old friends and made new ones. I will always cherish that time with my dad.

Thank you, Dad, for sharing your joy of exploring and your wonder for all the world's diversity and beauty.

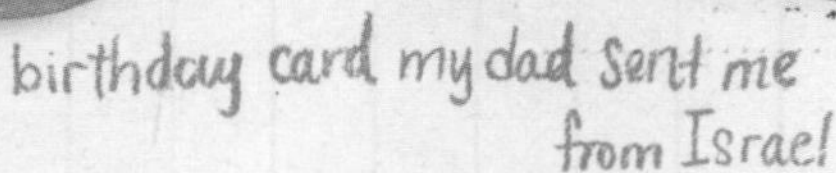

birthday card my dad sent me from Israel

ברכות ליום הולדתך

13

Happy Birthday

a savory Australian food paste

Three Sisters Rock Formation, Australia

Dad and me, Taos, New Mexico, 2018

Just like my dad, Lulu's papa carried home thoughtful treasures to share with his family. Many of his gifts are on the map below.

I wonder where you have visited. Where would you like to explore someday?